Diary
of
Steve the Noob
10

Steve the Noob

D0169979

Thanks to Rymdnisse for the rigs for the pictures.

Thank You

Thank you for picking up a copy of my book. I spent many hours putting this book together, so I hope that you will enjoy reading it. As a Minecraft player, it brings me great joy to be able to share my stories with you. The game is fun and entertaining, and surprisingly, writing about it can be almost just as fun. Once you are done reading this book, if you enjoyed it, please take a moment to leave a review. It will help other people discover this book. If after reading it, you realize that you hate it with such passion, please feel free to leave me a review anyway. I enjoy reading what people think about my books and writing style. I hope that many people will like this book and encourage me to keep writing. Thanks in advance.

Special thanks to readers of my previous books. Thank you for taking the time to leave a review. I appreciate it so much; your support means so much to me. I will continue to keep writing and will try to provide the highest quality of unofficial Minecraft books. Thank you for your support. If anyone needs to reach me, you can email me at steve.the.noob.diaries@gmail.com

3/4/2016

Thanks for the reviews and suggestions you all have been leaving me. Every time I read your reviews, it makes me smile, so thank you for that. You guys and girls have some great suggestions for the story line, I'll definitely take them into consideration as the series progress. I'm going to try to publish a new volume to this series every three weeks or so. Well, at least that's the plan. As for longer books, I don't know, I think my sweet spot is 8,000-9,000 words right now. Anyway, have fun reading #10. I guess I should go start on #11, huh?

Check Out My Author Page

Steve the Noob

My Other Books

Diary of Steve the Noob

Diary of Steve the Noob 2

Diary of Chester the Sheep

Iron Golem

The Librarian

Other Books

Tuesday

The smell of burning wood filled my nostrils. I opened my eyes to see my world on fire. My house was burning up, and I was tied to my bed. I couldn't move, I couldn't do a thing. Through the window, I could see my friend Joe running away from a mob of skeletons. They shot a bazillion arrows at him. *There's no way he was going to survive that*, I thought. The village was in turmoil, and I was completely helpless. The smoke filled my lungs... I couldn't breathe...

GASP!

My body twitched and I awoke in a shocked state. I sat up and took in a huge breath of air.

"What… was that…?" I said out loud as my heart pounded violently in my chest. Sweat was dripping from my face.

I looked around the room. Lucky was fast asleep in the corner. It was still night time, nothing was burning.

"Was I dreaming? Was that a nightmare…? Joe… the villagers…"

I laid back down on the floor and found that it was soaking wet. "Why is the floor all wet…?" Then I had a realization… "Oh, no… did I… did I pee my pants!?" I had to check… "Whew… I'm good, it probably got wet from my sweat…"

I sat up and sighed. "There's no way I can get back to sleep now…"

I got up and paced around the room a bit to try to calm myself down. Through the window, I noticed Devlin was walking around patrolling the streets.

"Ah, some fresh air… that should help." I opened the door and went outside.

The noise of the door closing caught Devlin's attention.

"W-who's there?" he asked in a nervous voice.

"It's just me, Steve."

"Whew… I thought it was a zombie or something. What are you doing out here during this time of night?"

"I couldn't sleep…"

"Really?" He walked up to me and noticed my face. "You look like you've seen a ghost or something. Are you okay?"

"I, um, had a really bad nightmare."

"About what?" he asked curiously.

"Err… I don't really want to talk about it…"

"Come on, you can talk to me. I won't tell anyone," he said.

"It is kinda personal, it is about my past."

"Did you dream about your old home?"

I looked at Devlin with a shocked expression. "You know about my first home?"

"Yeah, I read about it in a newspaper. There was a small column covering your interview."

"Oh… yeah…" I said hesitantly, "I was dreaming about it."

He nodded. "I figured as much. So, what happened?"

"Um…"

"You can tell me, there's no one here but us," Devlin said encouragingly. "I know we barely know one another, but if we are to be working together, we should be able to talk to each other."

That made a lot of sense to me, so I gave in. "Okay… in my dream, rather my nightmare, I lived through the disaster that took place in the village."

"Uh-huh…"

"What happened that night was I fell from a tower and was knocked unconscious, I didn't see what happened afterwards. But in my nightmare, I felt like I was living through it as it happened."

"I see… so, you got a glimpse of what you may have missed?"

"Yeah, that's pretty much it, plus some other random events and details like I couldn't move."

"That sounds like you felt powerless."

"Exactly! I couldn't help even if I wanted to."

"It's okay, it was just a dream. How are you feeling now?"

"I don't know… it got me thinking… what if I'm not good enough to defend this village? What if I fail again?"

Devlin smiled at me. "Steve, you've come a long way. If you were the same person as you were back then, I would definitely not have moved here."

I laughed meekly.

"You're much stronger now, and you've got friends to back you up."

I nodded.

"Whatever challenges you have to go through, you don't have to go through it alone. We got your back, Steve."

"Wow… thanks for your words of support, Devlin. I feel much better now."

"I'm glad to hear that."

"You know, I've only known you for a short amount of time, but yet I feel like you know me really well."

He smiled a big o' smile. "Well, to be honest, I am a big fan of yours. You are the main reason why I moved here."

"Really?" I said in a surprised voice.

"Yeah, I admire your work and goals. Your actions are noble and your heart is true."

"Wow… you gathered all that from the interview?"

Devlin laughed. "Partially, and from watching you interact with others."

I smiled. "Thanks, Devlin. I needed this talk."

"Anytime, Steve. Alright, I should keep patrolling."

"You know what, just take the rest of the night off. I'll cover your shift."

"What, really?"

"Yeah, I can't sleep anyway. Go on, I'm sure you're tired."

"Cool! Thanks, Steve."

"Oh! That reminds me, I must apologize now, I forgot to make beds for our new homes. Sorry about that."

He laughed. "That's okay, I don't mind sleeping on the floor."

"I'll go hunting for some sheep later today. Thanks again for the pep talk."

We waved goodbye and Devlin went to his new home.

I wasn't sure what time it was, but I was guessing maybe 4 or 5 A.M.

"The sun should be up soon," I said to myself as I walked around the outskirts of the village.

On the horizons, I could see mobs wandering around. I saw a few skeletons, but didn't catch their attention.

"I should really get that wall up soon. It is time to move on to the next phase of the village defense plan."

I walked by the town hall. "This is my home now, and I will not fail… not this time…"

Then I continued my patrol and came across the library. "Ah… Cindy, when are you going to wake up?" I said softly to myself.

The sun was starting to poke its head up on the horizon.

I yawned as I watched the sunrise. The zombies fried and the skeletons burned. I snickered to myself.

I continued walking and came by Bob's house. Then I saw something that made my blood boil. It was a stupid green slime!

"YOU! What are you doing here?! You're not welcome here!" I yelled.

It just continued bouncing along.

"Grr! Don't ignore me!" I yelled as I kicked the slime as hard as I could.

I was expecting to send it flying off over the trench, but instead it broke and split in two.

"Ugh! Now there's two of you?!"

They bounced along happily as though nothing had happened.

"That's it! Time to bring out the big boy!" I reached into my inventory and got out my special weapon, the Bone Basher.

"Y'all gunna git it!" I said as I cackled a bit.

I lifted the mighty weapon over my shoulder using both hands. I held it there for a few seconds while trying to aim at the small slime cubes. A few seconds later, I let the hammer drop.

Boom!

"Ha! Take that!" I yelled, then I struggled to lift up my weapon again. "Ugh… so heavy…"

I looked at where the weapon landed, and there was a huge hole. It had completely destroyed the grass block. Unfortunately, right next to the hole were the two slimes, still bouncing along.

"I missed?"

They were starting to bounce away.

"Oh, no, you don't!" I said as I chased after them slamming down the Bone Basher every chance I got.

Boom!

Boom!

Boom!

The ground was full of potholes now, and I was completely exhausted from wielding the heavy weapon.

Bob came out running. "Whoa! What's going on? What's that ruckus out here?"

"Hey… Bob…" I said as I tried to catch my breath.

"Steve? What are you doing?"

The slimes were nowhere in sight by now. It was just me and a bunch of holes in the ground. "Uh… I was trying to… smash something…"

"Oh… you made kind of a mess out there."

"Yeah… sorry about that…"

"Well, did you at least succeed in smashing it?"

"No… they were too fast… and I was too slow…"

Bob laughed. "Wait… let me guess… slime cubes?"

I became embarrassed. "Uh, what? No…"

He laughed even harder. "You suck at lying."

I sighed.

"Anyway, maybe you should try to get stronger, so that you can wield that weapon properly."

"Get stronger? How?"

"Um, I don't know. Maybe exercise, do some strength training."

"Hm… that's an interesting idea."

Bob walked over to me and picked up the Bone Basher with ease. "Since you're already here, you want to come in for breakfast?"

"Sure, that sounds like a great idea. I'm pretty hungry from all that smashing."

He handed the weapon back to me. I reached for it with one hand, but couldn't support the weight, so it dropped to the ground.

"Hmm…" he said. "Come on."

Bob prepared some chicken for us and we ate together on the dining table.

"I want to be strong like you, Bob."

Bob smiled. "Ah, that takes time and a lot of training. Strength isn't built overnight."

"I see. What if we built a gym or something? Then I could work out and get stronger."

"That's not a bad idea," he said.

"And we could use it as a training ground for sparring, too."

"Ah, you want to keep your skills sharp, huh?"

"Well, that and I kinda want to train our new night guard. He should be able to defend himself and others if the need arises."

"Yes, that's true. Maybe you should run it by the mayor first?"

"Hmm…" I thought for a bit. "Nah, I think I can just do it," I said with a grin.

"Ah, right, you're the deputy mayor now, huh? It is going to take me awhile to get used to that."

I laughed. "Hey, what are you doing today?"

"Just going to work at the shop. Are you planning to build the training grounds today?"

"Yeah, but I guess whenever you have time."

"I'll let you know when I'm free."

"Hm… that reminds me, I should be building something else instead of this training ground."

"Build what?"

"I want to use all the stone blocks we gathered from our adventure and build a wall surrounding the whole village."

"Ah, that's a good idea, but it will take some time."

"Yeah, definitely."

"Alright, bud, I have to go to work now. I'll catch you later."

After leaving Bob's house, I walked over to the trench. "Well, nothing else to do but to get started, I guess."

I started laying down the foundation of the stone wall that would protect us from intruders.

I think I'll just make it two blocks high for now. That should be enough to keep out those pesky slimes and skeletons, I thought.

As I was working, a new villager approached me.

"Hello, Steve the Monster Hunter."

I turned around to see who it was. "Hi, I'm sorry, we haven't met."

"It is my pleasure to meet you, my name is Tommy."

"Hey, Tommy, are you new to this village?"

"Yep! Just moved here this morning."

"Really?"

"Yeah, I talked to the mayor and he told me to look for you."

"Oh?"

"He said you would help me get settled in and find a job and such."

"Ah… I see. Okay, great. This might work out quite well, then."

"What do you mean?"

"Well, we have one job opening right now," I said and smiled.

Tommy nodded. "Great, what is it?"

"We need a wall builder. Just take over what I was doing."

"You want to build this thing around the whole village?"

"Yep! I'll pay you one emerald a week."

"I guess that doesn't seem too hard."

"Nope, not at all," I said as I handed him hundreds of stone blocks. "Here, hang on to these. I gotta go build you a house."

"Oh, okay."

"You got it from here right?"

"Yeah, just build the wall behind this trench?"

"Yep! Two blocks high," I said as I walked off. "Oh, and welcome to our village, Tommy!"

Neat! I got someone to take care of the wall for me. Now, I can go handle other tasks, like building some beds, I thought to myself.

I walked into the fields looking for some sheep to slay. There weren't any in sight, but that wasn't going to stop me. I refused to sleep on the cold, hard floor again tonight. So further I journeyed into the green, flat fields in search of the fluffy, puffy animals.

Finally, I found some on the horizon. *YES! No floor for me tonight!* I thought. I ran towards them and drew out my heavy weapon. *These animals are big and slow, so they shouldn't be able to dodge my attacks.*

I lifted the Bone Basher over my head and slammed it down into the flock of sheep as hard as I could.

Boom!

It poofed a sheep in one strike, but spooked of the rest. They suffered a bit of damage from the shock of the attack. Because the weapon was so big and powerful, it causes minor AOE damage.

The rest of the flock scattered everywhere.

Aw, man! I can't chase down all those sheep with this big o' weapon, I thought and sighed. *Maybe I should reserve the big weapon for bigger enemies, and use a small weapon for smaller enemies.*

I drew out a stone sword and got to work on the sheep. I wished I had my iron sword, but it broke during the fight with the Skeleton King.

The sheep ran around in a panic as I whacked them as hard as I could. *I wish Lucky was here, he would have chased down all these sheep for me.*

After a few minutes of running around, the job was done. *Alright! Time to build some beds and a new house for Tommy.*

I headed back to the village. When I arrived, I was greeted by Lisa.

"Hello, Steve. Where are you off to?"

"Hi, Lisa. I'm just running some errands."

"Do you have a few minutes to chat with an elderly woman?"

"Of course, what's up?"

"Have you visited Cindy today yet?"

"No…" I looked down at the ground. "I'll try to stop by later."

She smiled. "Don't worry, dear, she'll be alright."

"You think so?"

"Yes, as a matter of fact, I'm going to go help Emily take care of her."

"Oh, you will? Thanks, Lisa," I said and smiled.

"It is no problem. I know you are quite busy now with your new job."

I laughed weakly. "Yeah, lots to do."

"Well, just focus on your work and leave Cindy to me. I don't want you to worry about her, you have enough on your plate already."

"Thank you." *Lisa is so nice and considerate,* I thought.

"I heard you hired a new guard?"

I nodded. "Yes, Devlin is his name."

"That's good, dear, the villagers can sleep more soundly at night."

"I was thinking that, too."

"If you are focusing more on villager safety, have you put any more thought into a village guardian?"

"Oh, you mean the iron golem?"

"Yes, having that guardian would definitely make the villagers feel safer."

I scratched my head a bit. "I haven't really put too much thought into it, no."

"Well, you found a lot of iron from your trip, didn't you? You can make a guardian," Lisa said with hopeful eyes.

"Yeah… about that, I think we used up most of the iron to make the rail tracks."

Lisa looked sad. "Oh, I see…"

I didn't mean to disappoint her. "B-but don't worry, I'm sure we'll get an iron golem soon!"

She looked up with a half smile. "I hope so, too… I've wasted enough of your time already. You should go complete your tasks. Thanks for entertaining this old woman."

"It was fun talking to you, Lisa."

We waved and I was on my way home.

Gee… iron sure is super useful around here. Ugh… but I really don't want to go all the way back to that mining place.

I arrived home and started working on Tommy's house. I attached his house right next to Devlin's to save time and material. It didn't take too long to finish building it and our beds. I left the extra beds out in front of the houses for Tommy and Devlin.

Whew! I'm exhausted. It has been a long day; I think I'm gonna hit the hay early.

I walked to my door and opened it. Lucky came flying out, I guess he was bored from being cooped up in the house all day.

"Whoa! Where are you going?"

He just ran off and did his thing.

"I'm going to bed! You might have to sleep outside tonight!" I yelled, as if he understood me.

I placed down my new bed in my new house. The smell of new wool filled the house. My body flopped on the bed and I was knocked out.

Wednesday

    I woke up the next morning to some scratching on my door and whining. "Ugh… what's that? Who's there?" I said groggily.

    The whining and scratching continued.

    I finally got up and opened the door.

    Lucky came rushing in. He was shaking and whining.

    "Hey, boy, are you okay? Was it too cold out there?"

    He whined some more.

    "Aw… poor doggy. If only I could build a fire or something." Then I looked in my inventory and realized that I had tons of stone blocks. So, I built a furnace and placed it near Lucky.

    "Here you go, boy. Sorry about keeping you outside," I said as I petted him. I threw in a couple of wooden planks to start the fire.

    Lucky snuggled up to the furnace.

"Don't get too close. You don't wanna burn off all of your fur, do you?"

He rolled his eyes at me.

"Alright, I'm gonna head out, don't burn the house down, okay?"

Before I left the house, I put some raw steaks on the floor for my pet. As for me, I headed outside with some carrots in my hands. It was a cloudy day, kind of chilly. It looked like it might rain.

"Hmm… maybe Lucky had the right idea about staying inside cuddled up next to a warm fire," I said to myself.

"Yep, might be a cold one," a voice said.

I turned to my side and saw Devlin. "Hey, how did the night patrol go?"

"Ez-pz, nothing to report."

"That's good to hear. I was thinking that we need to get you some gear and training soon."

"Really?" he said excitedly.

"Yeah, I want you to look the part. People will be looking to you for protection."

"Kinda like how they look to you."

"Yeah, I guess so."

"Well, I'm looking forward to it… to train under the great Monster Hunter."

I chuckled. "Alright, bud, go get some shut eye."

I wandered the empty street for a bit, then I came across Bob.

"Hey, you're up early," I said.

"Yeah, just trying to get in some exercise before work."

"Oh, I didn't know you were into the fitness thing."

"Nah, I just like walking in the morning. Why are you up so early?"

"Oh… heh." I told Bob about how I left Lucky outside last night.

"Wow, that's mean," he said and laughed.

"Ah, it is just bad timing."

Then Bob remembered something. "Oh! Did Lisa talk to you?"

"She talked to you, too?"

"Yes, it seems she really wants an iron golem for our village."

I nodded. "But we don't have enough iron."

"The mayor spoke to me about this issue as well."

"He did?"

"Yeah, he likes her idea and wants you to make it happen."

"Whuuuuut?" I was shocked. "I'm not going back there!"

Bob chuckled. "Luckily, you don't have to."

I had this confused look on my face. "What do you mean…?"

"I'll be going there to mine."

I shook my head in disbelief. "No way, by yourself?"

"If I have to, yeah."

"That's way too dangerous!" I yelled.

"It's okay, you've trained me well," he said and smiled.

"Ugh, we just came from that place and now you're planning to go back?"

"Yeah, but unlike you, I love mining."

"That's true…"

"Anyway, I'll probably leave in a few days or in a week."

"Wait, this is happening too quickly. Give me some time to process this before anything."

"Alright, Steve, but either way, I'm going."

We went our separate ways.

I can't believe Bob would risk his life again after just barely coming home. He has become a real adventurer, I thought to myself. *He seems rather quite stubborn on the issue, too.*

I didn't have anything planned for the day, so I decided to go help Tommy build the wall. When I arrived at the wall, I saw that Tommy was quite productive yesterday. At this rate, the wall might be finished in under a week.

"Ah, this is coming along nicely," I said to myself, as I got out some stone blocks from my inventory.

I continued working on the wall for the next few hours.

Tommy came by and helped me shortly after. Together, we worked side by side and built our village defensive wall. We were working so hard and diligently that I totally lost track of time.

"Alright, Tommy, I'm gonna head out."

"Okay, Steve, I got it from here."

I headed back home to check up on Lucky. He came bursting out of the door again.

I laughed. "Bored again?"

He ran off and disappeared again.

"Ugh… I guess I'll have to wait for him to come home tonight."

I had some time to spare, so I went to the library to visit Cindy.

Emily greeted me as I entered the library. "Hey, Steve. Sorry, Cindy is still sleeping."

"Oh, I just wanted to see her," I said.

"Lisa is in the back with her."

I walked into the small room.

"Hey, Lisa, whatcha up to?"

"Steve? What are you doing here? Don't you have work to do?"

I scratched my head. "Uh, yeah, I guess, but I just wanted to see Cindy."

"Well, as you can see, same o', same o'," she said.

"I see…" I stared at our sleeping Cindy for a bit.

"Go on about your business. You don't need to be here."

"You're taking good care of her?"

"You bet. I'm about to brush her teeth, brush her hair, and such."

"Okay," I said as I walked away slowly. "Thanks, Lisa."

It was good to see Cindy, even though she wasn't doing anything. It is just nice to see that she was a regular looking villager again. I left the library and patrolled the village for a bit.

Nighttime was here and Lucky was nowhere in sight, so I stayed out for a bit longer. I saw Devlin leave his house to start his shift. Tommy was tired from building all day, so he went home to rest.

I walked around and saw some skeletons near the trench. *Hmm… this could be trouble. Maybe I should clear them out,* I thought.

I approached the trench and one of the skeletons noticed me. He let loose an arrow straight at my face.

I drew out my stone sword and turned it flat to block the arrow. "Whoa… what an aggressive bonehead."

The other skeletons turned to look at me. There was not much time for me to think, so I acted fast. I jumped over the trench and dashed towards the group of skeletons.

They hailed a barrage of arrows towards me, and I did my best to block them with my sword.

Ting!

Ting!

Ting!

Every arrow that I blocked or struck me pushed me back further and further away from those walking white sticks.

Ugh!

I was frustrated that I couldn't close the distance on them, so I threw my stone sword at them in anger.

"GRRR!! Take this!"

Of course, the sword only a few blocks from where I was, but now I didn't have a weapon.

"Oops…"

They continued to fire shots after shots at me.

I ducked and weaved and tried so hard to dodge, but I couldn't escape all the arrows. My hearts were running low. I had to retreat.

So, I tucked tail and ran back towards the village.

The skeletons tried to chase me down; they followed me until they fell into the trench.

I turned back to look and saw that they were stuck in the ditch. "HA! You fell into my trap!"

I limped over to the trench. "That was my plan all along…"

Right when I peeked into the trench, the skeletons shot arrows upward at me. The arrows missed me by inches. "Whoa… these skinnys have got to go."

From my inventory, I pulled out the Bone Basher. "Oh, yeaaaaaah! This baby was made for this!"

I lifted my huge weapon over my head and slammed it into the trench.

Boom!

All I could hear afterward was the sound of bones clattering and dropping to the ground. I took a peek into the trench; there was nothing left but a pile of bones down there.

"Haha! Take that, fools!" I yelled.

At this time, Devlin noticed me by the trench and came over.

"Steve! Are you alright?!"

"Yeah…" I said weakly.

"But you're covered in arrows!"

"What, this? This is nothing… barely a scratch…" I said as I did my best to play it off cool.

"Come on, let's get you home. I'll help you."

"It's okay, I got it," I said as I tried to walk straight, but a few arrows had struck my legs.

Devlin inspected my leg wounds closer. "Whoa… you took an arrow to your knee. Are you going to be okay? Are your adventuring days over now?"

I laughed. "Pfft… I'm gonna walk it off," I said as I limped off slowly.

"Such a beast…" Devlin whispered.

I grinned as I made my way home.

As soon as I got out of Devlin's sight, my limp became way worse.

Ahhh… I can't believe I got shot in the knee! This hurts so much! But gotta make it home, I thought to myself. I started pulling out the arrows from my body. *At least I got some arrows out of that fight. These will come in handy later, I'm sure.* I gathered, maybe, something like 15 arrows. Yeah, I got shot… *a lot.*

When I arrived at my front door, I saw that Lucky was there waiting for me.

"Finally back, huh?"

Woof?

"Oh, this? I fought some skeletons… coulda used your help…"

Woof!

"I *tried* to dodge, but there were just too many arrows coming at me."

Woof…

I sighed. "Come on, let's go inside. I need to eat and rest to recover from these injuries."

Again, I gave Lucky some raw steaks and I ate carrots while laying on my bed. I was lazy and injured, so I didn't feel like preparing new food.

As I laid there, I kept thinking about those skeletons and their arrows.

Hmm… if only I could design something that could block those arrows, then I could just gather the arrows for later usage. Something like a shield would work, but how do I build a shield? Hmm… I know! I'll ask our blacksmith tomorrow.

I fell asleep shortly after.

Thursday

The next morning, I went to visit Bob at his house immediately. I was super excited about my idea. A shield would protect me and help me gather arrows. It is win-win.

I explained to Bob about my idea.

"Hmm… that's a good idea, Steve."

"Yeah, I think so, too."

"What should we make it out of?"

"Something sturdy, but not too heavy. I want to be able to carry it with one hand."

"Ah… well, definitely wood, then. I'll probably throw in a bit of metal too to make it extra beefy."

"Sounds like a plan."

"Come on, let's head to the workshop and try out some designs."

Together, we headed to the blacksmith shop. We tried different configurations for the shield using a crafting table. I tried filling all the slots with wood planks, but didn't work. Bob tried all wood planks with an iron ingot in the middle, that didn't work either.

After a few hours and many, many tries, we found a configuration that worked. The recipe was a "Y" shape made of wood planks, and an iron ingot in between the opening of the "Y". The shield came out looking mighty sturdy. The face was mostly wood and the handle was made of metal.

"Wow! This thing looks cool!" I said.

"Yeah, it isn't too heavy, either."

"I can't wait to go test it on some skeletons."

Bob laughed. "Okay, just be careful out there."

"I think I'm gonna take Devlin with me. We'll get some training in."

Bob looked concerned. "Are you sure? That might be a bit harsh of an introduction to combat."

"Eh… it should be fine. We'll be right by the village, plus I have this shield now."

"Alright, bud, your call. I should probably go back to work now."

I laughed. "Sorry to keep ya. Thanks, Bob."

When I left the blacksmith shop, the time was around 3 P.M. I had some time to kill before nighttime, so I went to an empty part of the village.

"I think I'll build the training grounds here," I said to myself.

I started building some fences for the enclosure.

"Ah, gotta make room for workout equipment, too."

I laid down the foundation for the training grounds. It was 20 x 20 blocks big. Because it was so big, I had to re-dig the trench to accommodate the new structure.

The sun was about to set soon, and a new villager approached me.

"Hi, I was told to come find you. My name is Calvin."

"Hiya, are you another new settler here?"

"Yup!"

"Will you be needing a job, Calvin?"

"Well, at my old village, I was a hunter, so I can keep doing that here if you want."

"A hunter? That's interesting."

"Yeah, I would just go around and hunt for food."

"So you have combat experience?"

Calvin nodded. "A bit…"

"What kind of weapon do you use?"

Calvin pulled out his weapon. "Bow and arrows."

My eyes lit up. "Ooooh… I used to be an archer, too."

He laughed. "Yeah, it is fun, but arrows are hard to come by."

"Yeah! I ran out of arrows and just gave it up. How do you get arrows?"

"Oh, I trade for them, or sometimes I make them myself."

"I see…" I thought for a moment. "Well, since our village is growing, I guess we'll be needing more food. So, you can continue being a hunter if you want."

Calvin smiled. "Yeah, that would be great!"

"You're gonna need a place to sleep."

"Oh, don't worry about me, I like to sleep outside."

"You do?"

"Yep! I'm an outdoors type of person. I'm actually trying to become a ranger."

"A ranger? What's that?"

"You don't know what a ranger is?"

I shook my head.

"Well, it is the next class above an archer. Rangers are one with the wilderness. When you become a ranger, you get cool new survivor skills and become quite deadly with a bow."

"Really? That sounds interesting."

"I'm surprised you never heard of the ranger class before. What class are you?"

"W-wha?"

"You don't know your class?"

"I have no idea what you're talking about, sorry."

"N-no… that's okay…" he said, then he muttered something to himself, "I guess he really is a noob…"

"What? Did you say something?"

"Ahem! N-no, no… I think you heard the wind blowing."

"Um, okay. Well, I'll leave you to it, then. Welcome to the village, Calvin."

"Thanks, Steve."

We shook hands and parted ways.

I headed back to my house to let Lucky out. Also, I had to wait for Devlin to come out, so that we could start our training and testing of the shield.

Lucky came flying out as usual.

"Maybe I should build you a little doggy house out here, so that you can come and go as you please."

Wooooof! He barked as he ran all over the place.

I looked into my inventory to see what kind of material I wanted to use for the doggy house.

Before I could decide, Devlin came out from his house.

"Hey, Steve, what's up?"

I filled him in on everything.

"T-that's sounds a bit dangerous, but okay… let's go," he said nervously.

"Don't worry, I'll be right by your side," I said, trying my best to reassure him.

Together, we headed over the trench and into monster territory. I gave him a stone sword and equipped one myself.

"Okay, let's go find some skeletons," I said.

"S-skeletons? Shouldn't we start off with something small… like, maybe, a rabbit or something?"

"A rabbit?" I laughed. "Nah, don't worry. I'm gonna pick up all the aggro, all you have to do is swing."

"Really? It is that easy?"

"Yup!" I said and then spotted a lone skeleton archer. "There! Come on, let's go…"

"O-okay…"

We approached the unsuspecting skeleton.

"Okay, get down low, crouch and use your sneak mode. I don't want you to get his attention."

Devlin nodded.

I stood tall and even jumped a bit, trying to get aggro from the skeleton.

Finally, he noticed me and shot an arrow my way.

I raised up my shield.

Thud!

"Ha! It works! It blocked the arrow completely."

"Sweet… now what?" said Devlin.

The skeleton fired another arrow.

Thud!

"This is awesome. I'm not even getting pushed back. This is a total game changer," I said.

"Are we just gonna keep staying here?"

"No, we're gonna advance on the skeleton, then you're gonna whack him good with your sword."

"O-okay… I'm ready…"

Thud!

Thud!

Thud!

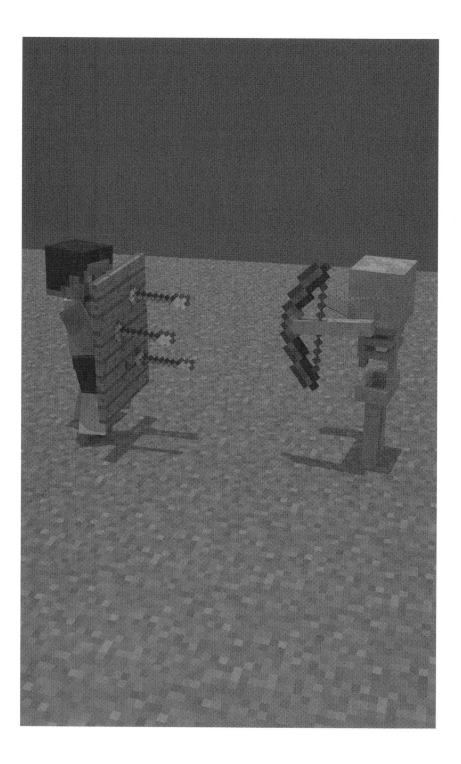

We made our way to the archer. I was standing right in front of him, blocking his shots.

"Alright, stand to the side of me and hit him, but keep behind the shield."

Devlin did as I instructed.

The skeleton flinched and flashed red.

"Keep doing it, keep going."

Devlin swung a few more times and the skeleton poofed.

"Nice! Good job, Devlin."

"Whoa… that felt… *AMAZING!!*"

I laughed.

"I'm getting such a rush from this! Maybe I was born for battle!" he yelled.

I smiled, then looked around. I noticed a green armless creature approaching us.

"Oh, no!" I said.

"What? What's wrong?"

"It's that creature! The one that blows up!"

"Blows up?!" he yelled.

"Come on! Let's run! I don't want to fight that thing up close."

"Okay, lead the way!"

We both turned around and ran for it.

Devlin was panicky while he was running. He tripped and fell to the ground.

Oof!

I turned around to see him on the ground with the creeper closing in.

"Devlin! Get up!" I yelled.

He got up and started limping. "Ahh! I think I sprained my ankle!"

The creeper was catching up to him.

Uh-oh… it is fight or die now, I thought as I ran back towards him.

"Go on without me, Steve!"

"No! I'm not leaving you!"

The creeper was right next to him and it started to expand.

Sssssssssss…

Devlin looked right at the green monster. He closed his eyes, I think he knew what was coming next.

I jumped right in between the creeper and Devlin and raised my shield to protect the both of us.

BOOOOM!

A close impact explosion. The force sent me and Devlin flying a few blocks away.

Ugh!

Oof!

My ears were ringing and my vision was blurry, but a few blocks from me, I could make out the shape of Devlin's body. Immediately, I rolled over to him to see how he was doing.

"Devlin! Are you okay?"

There was no response…

"Hey! Can you hear me?" I asked as I poked him.

He felt kind of squishy and fluffy…

"Wha… wait, why are you so fluffy?"

Then I realized it…

Baaaaaaa…

I had mistaken a brown sheep for Devlin.

"Steve, I'm over here…" Devlin said weakly.

I turned to my right and saw another blurry figure on the ground. "Are you okay?"

Cough… "Yeah, I think so… I think your shield saved us."

"Yeah… I think it did, too… but where is it?"

"I don't know…"

"Maybe it disintegrated from the blast?"

"Possibly…"

I came over to him and helped him up. "Come on, let's get home. It is too dangerous out here in our current conditions."

"Yeah, enough training for tonight…"

We limped back to the village.

"Thanks for saving me, Steve. You're a true friend."

"I'm sure you would have done the same for me."

"Yeah, no doubt."

Out of nowhere, Calvin came dashing towards us.

"Are you guys alright?! I heard an explosion… a creeper from the sound of it."

I was surprised by his awareness and knowledge. "Yeah, we're okay," I replied. "It was a close run in."

"What happened?" he asked.

I explained to Calvin what had just happened.

"Next time, carry a range weapon with you. Creepers are best fought from afar."

"Good idea. I'll build myself a bow tomorrow," I said.

"Are you guys going to be alright from here?" he asked.

"I think so," said Devlin.

"Okay, I'm gonna go back to sleep."

I scratched my head. "By the way, where are you sleeping tonight?"

"I made a nice spot for myself high up in a tree."

"Is it comfortable?"

"It does the trick, plus it gives me a nice view of the surrounding area."

"Oooh… it is kinda like a watch tower."

Calvin nodded. "A bit, yeah."

"Okay, we gotta get home. Thanks for coming out to check on us."

"You got it. See ya." Calvin stayed behind for a bit with his bow at the ready. I guess he wanted to make sure that there would be no more ambushes tonight.

Ten minutes later, we made it back to our triplex home. It took kind of long because we were limping the whole way. Lucky was outside waiting for me again.

He whined as we approached. He was probably thinking, "What on Minecraftia happened to you guys?"

"Okay, Devlin, you should eat and rest up tonight."

He groaned a bit. "Ugh… no, it is my shift. I need to patrol the village."

"It's okay, you can skip this one night. You're in no condition to be walking around much right now."

Devlin sighed. "I guess you're right…"

"Alright, good night. I'll see you tomorrow for some more training…"

"What?! More training?!"

I laughed. "Just kidding…"

"Whew…"

"I think…"

"Huh?"

"Later, bud," I said as I went into my house.

It felt so good to be home. The first thing I did was sat down on my bed. "Whew… what a day…" Then I looked in my inventory for some food.

"What?! Carrots again?! Come on… we really need to hire a village chef to prepare food for everyone."

Lucky sighed.

"You know what, let's trade tonight, boy. I'll eat the raw steak and you can have the carrots."

My pet just hung his head low to the floor.

"What? You don't like veggies? They are good for you!"

Now he flopped his body to the ground, like he's dying.

"Fine! Have your steaks!" I said bitterly as I bit on a carrot.

He happily devoured the raw steaks.

I sighed as I chewed on the carrots.

"At least we know the shield works. We're definitely gonna need more of those."

Lucky just munched away.

He makes the steaks look so good. I guess carrots wouldn't be so bad if there was something to dip them in. Maybe something like ranch sauce or peanut butter, I thought to myself.

I laid down after finishing my raw carrots, and fell asleep before I even knew it.

Friday

I woke up extra late in the day. I think my body was just exhausted from the beatings I've been taking. Lucky was sleeping there right along with me. *Man, this wolf is a little piggy, too! It's not just me,* I thought to myself and laughed.

"Okay, time to get the day started."

We left the house, and Lucky ran off to go play or whatever it is he does.

"Just make sure to come back before night time!" I yelled at my pet as he ran off.

I went over to Devlin's house and knocked on his door.

Devlin opened the door looking quite refreshed. "Hey, Steve. How are you feeling today?"

"Much better," I said and laughed. "Are you ready for more training?"

Devlin's eyes grew big. "What? I thought you were kidding…"

"Come on, we gotta get you in tip-top shape if you are to defend this village."

"Um, I don't know, last night was a bit too dangerous."

I nodded. "Yeah, but don't worry, we'll be training in the village today."

"What do you have in mind?"

I smiled. "Come on, I'll show you!"

I started jogging towards the training ground, which was behind our homes. Devlin followed closely behind me.

"Here, look! I built this for us…"

"You built some fences for us?" Devlin asked.

"What? No, it is a training ground!"

"It is? Oh… if you say so…" he said with uncertainty.

"We can practice techniques and spar inside."

"I see… this would be way safer than yesterday."

"Yeah, probably."

"We should have started here first, Steve."

"Meh… where is the fun in that?"

"But you gotta learn to walk before you can run."

"We did okay yesterday, didn't we?"

Devlin shook his head. "We almost died…"

I felt guilty when he said that, but I laughed to try to cover it up. "Sorry, I needed to test the shield last night. I figured I could train you, too. It would be like hitting two birds with one stone."

"Oh…"

"I had no idea that a creeper would show up out of nowhere. I'll try to be more careful in the future."

"It's okay… we made it out alive."

"Yep!" I said as I stretched. "Now, come on, let's go over some basic sword techniques."

"Okay, now that's the type of training I was looking forward to."

I made wooden swords for the both of us, and then I explained to Devlin the different techniques such as thrusting, slashing, and parrying. Together, we practiced for the next hour.

"Whew… I'm breaking a sweat," Devlin said.

"Yeah, me too."

"This is a great workout, and I'm learning so much."

"Yeah, you're progressing pretty fast," I said, then I had an idea. "Hey, stay here. I'm gonna go somewhere, I'll be back."

"Oh? What should I do in the meantime?"

"Keep practicing."

"With what?"

"Hmm…" I thought for a bit, then I crafted a wooden dummy doll. "Here, practice on this while I'm gone."

"Okay!" he said enthusiastically.

Hmm… he still has a good amount of energy left. We might end up training all day, I thought.

I left the training grounds and headed over to Bob's work place.

"Hey, Steve! How did the shield testing go yesterday?"

"It was awesome! It worked so well that I'm here to ask for two more."

Bob laughed. "It was *that* good, huh?"

"Yeah, also, I know we are tight on iron, but can you craft me an iron helmet?"

"A helmet? Sure, no problem. We gotta keep our deputy mayor well protected, right?"

"Well, it isn't for me. It is for Devlin. I want him to have some gear."

"Ah, I see. Yeah, I think we have enough iron for two shields and a helmet."

"Great!"

"Give me a few minutes and I'll have you on your way."

Bob disappeared into the shop. Flames roared from the forge. I think he was smelting the iron ores to turn them into ingots. Then I heard lots of banging and clattering coming from the shop. A few moments later, Bob returned with the items I requested.

"Here you go, Steve. May they serve you well."

"Thanks, Bob. What do I owe you for these?"

"For you? On the house, Steve," he said and waved.

"Thanks, you're the best!" I said as I left.

I returned to the training grounds and found Devlin swinging at the dummy I made.

"Nice swing! Good form!" I said.

"You're back? Where did you go?" Devlin asked as he wiped the sweat from his face.

"Here, I got you something."

"You did? What is it?"

"Consider it as part of your guard uniform," I said as I handed him the iron helmet.

"Whoa… this is for me? Are you sure?"

I nodded. "Yeah, of course."

"But you don't even have a helmet yourself, maybe you should wear this."

I laughed. "No, no, I want everyone to know you're our guard. You need to look the part."

"Wow, thanks, Steve," he said and then placed the helmet on his head. "It fits me well."

I smiled. "I have one more thing for you."

His eyes grew big. "You do?"

"Yep! Here…" I gave him his own shield. "Now you'll really look like a guard."

"Wow… I don't know what to say…" Devlin looked at the ground. "I don't have anything to give to you."

I chuckled. "Don't worry about it, consider it my apology for endangering your life yesterday. It was a mistake on my part for taking you out there."

"O-oh… I see… w-well, I always felt safe yesterday. I mean, I was with the Slime Slayer after all. I knew you would protect me."

I smiled. "I'm glad we made it out okay, but please accept my apology."

Devlin looked up at me. "O-of course!" he said nervously.

"Great, thank you. With this new gear, you can now protect yourself and others."

"Okay, Steve. I won't let you down, thank you."

"Come on, let's get back to training."

It was then that Emily arrived.

"Heya, boys. Whatcha up to?"

"Hey, Emily. We're just training. What brings you out here?" I asked.

"Oh, I got bored at the library. With Lisa there taking care of Cindy, I don't have much else to do."

"Oh… wanna watch us train?" asked Devlin.

"Sure, that sounds fun. You don't mind if I take some notes, do you guys?"

"Notes?"

"Yeah, maybe I'll write a book about combat training one day."

"Ah, go ahead," I said.

"Doesn't bother me," our night guard replied.

Devlin and I equipped our new shields and continued sparring with one another. We practiced different shield techniques like bashing, blocking, and rushing. It was great to have someone to practice with. We continued to spar for about an hour until a stranger arrived.

"You! I know you!" the outsider yelled.

The three of us turned to look across the trench.

"You're Steve! That noob that destroyed my village!"

The three of us were shocked.

"I'm sorry… who are you?" I asked.

"You're Steve, aren't you? That jerk that burned down my village!"

"I… I am… Steve, yes… you're a villager from my first home?"

"I've finally found you… I heard about you escaping to another village. What are you trying to do here? Are you trying to destroy this village, too?!"

"Wha- what? No! I don't purposely go around trying to destroy villages!"

The stranger turned to address Emily. "What did he tell you? Did you say he wants to protect you?!"

"Um…" Emily stalled.

"He did say that, didn't he?! Don't believe him! He's a noob! A big noob! He's gonna burn down your house!"

"Uh… whoa… maybe you should chill out," Devlin said.

"Shut up, boy! You don't know Steve like I do!"

"All I know is that Steve is our hero. He is Steve the Monster Hunter," Devlin replied.

"Pfft! *Monster Hunter?*" the man cackled. "No, you should call him Steve the Destroyer… *of Villages!*"

All this yelling and complaining started to attract the attention of other villagers.

"You villagers! Don't listen to Steve's lies! He's a liar *and* a noob!" the stranger yelled into the crowd.

Everyone gasped and murmured among themselves.

"He says he wants to protect the village, but he's not worthy! He's just a noob!" the angry man shouted.

At this point, Devlin got mad, he couldn't take it anymore. "You! Get out of here! Go home!"

The stranger cackled. "Go home?! Home?! I don't have a home! Thanks to your *hero*."

I stumbled a few steps towards the angry outsider. "I-I'm sorry for the pain that I caused you, but it was not intentional..." I said.

"Pfffft! Tell that to the other villagers that were lost that night!" the man screamed.

"I-I really did try my best that night to protect the town... but we got swarmed and I was overwhelmed..."

"Excuses! I will not listen to the excuses of a noob!"

The mayor arrived at this point. "What's going on? What's causing all this commotion?"

Emily told the mayor what was going on.

Once the mayor understood the situation, he put on his serious face. "You there!" he said and pointed to the stranger. "Leave these premises immediately," he said in a strong, stern voice.

"No! It's a free world, I'll do whatever I want!" the man yelled back.

The mayor looked upset. "Devlin!"

"Y-yes, sir!" Devlin immediately stood straight at attention.

"Get rid of that intruder. Do whatever you have to."

"Yes, sir!" Devlin ran over to the trench with weapon and shield at the ready.

"Wait, is violence really necessary?" I asked.

"If it needs to be," the mayor said coldly, "I will not have this stranger causing unrest in my village."

"He's been through a lot, I don't think we should hurt him," I said to the mayor.

"He's hurting your reputation and spewing nonsense. We need to get rid of him. There are no other options," he replied firmly.

Whoa… I've never seen the mayor like this before. He's so serious, I thought.

Devlin ran towards the stranger.

"What?! You think I'm afraid of you, boy?! Bring it!" the man yelled.

"I'm asking you to leave one more time before things get physical!" Devlin yelled.

"AHHHHHH!" the man screamed as he rushed towards our new guard.

Devlin's heart was pounding like mad, but he managed to raise his shield and push away the charging man. "Get out of here!" Devlin yelled as he gave the man a shield bash to the face.

Bup!

Oof!

The stranger fell to his feet.

Devlin hovered over him and raised his wooden sword in the air.

"Ahh! N-no, no… okay, I'll leave…" the mysterious man said.

"That's right! You better get out of here!"

He got up slowly and walked away.

We all looked at him as he left.

Then he turned around and yelled, "Steve is a noob! Don't believe what he says!"

Devlin got mad and chased after him, but the stranger sprinted away.

"Get out of here! I hope the monsters get you on your way home!" Devlin yelled.

The crowd watched the man sprinted away and whispered to themselves.

"Alright, that's done and over with. He was just some crazy guy wandering the plains," said the mayor. "Come on, back to your businesses, people."

I stood there in shock because of what had just happened.

"Are you okay, Steve?" Devlin asked as he returned to us.

"Y-yeah… I think so…"

"Don't mind him, he's just some jerk."

I didn't say anything.

"We need to keep an eye out for that guy. I have a feeling he'll be back," said the mayor.

"That was weird… and disruptive," said Emily.

"Sorry," I said.

"Sorry? For what?" asked the mayor.

"I don't know… I'm gonna go home now."

"What? But what about our training?" Devlin asked.

"Sorry, I just don't really feel like training right now…" I said.

"Don't let that guy get to you, son," said the mayor. "He doesn't know what he was talking about."

"But that's the thing… maybe he does," I said and looked down at the ground, "what if he's right?"

"Do not doubt yourself. You are this village's hero, and we need you to be strong and confident."

I turned away from everyone. "I just want to be alone right now," I said as I left.

"Steve…" Emily tried to say something, but I kept walking.

"Let him go," the mayor said. "He needs time to himself."

They watched me as I walked home.

When I arrived at my house, Lucky was at the front door sleeping.

It must be nice to go play all day and then sleep afterward, I thought.

I opened the door and let him inside. Immediately, I collapsed on my bed and a gazillion thoughts ran through my mind. *What if that man was right? What if I'm just a noob who is in way over his head? What if I fail to protect the villagers here, too?*

So many questions, they seemed endless. *What am I doing here? I'm supposed to stop the monster problem that plagues this land. Where did I come from? Who am I?*

My head spiraled out of control. I tried to go to sleep, but I just kept tossing and turning. The stranger's words haunted me, and my night became restless. I just laid in bed for hours, just thinking.

I need to find some answers...

Through my window, I could see the sky change colors. It was completely dark, but then it started to become light blue.

I closed my eyes. *When I wake up, I will find some answers. Somehow, some way, I'll find some answers.*

Can You Help Me Out?

Thanks for reading all the way through. I hope that you enjoyed this book. As a new writer, it is hard to get started; it is difficult to find an audience that wants to read my books. There are millions of books out there and sometimes it is super hard to find one specific book. But that's where you come in! You can help other readers find my books by leaving a simple review. It doesn't have to be a lengthy or well written review; it just has to be a few words and then click on the stars. It would take less than 5 minutes.

Seriously, that would help me so much, you don't even realize it. Every time I get a review, good or bad, it just fills me with motivation to keep on writing. It is a great feeling to know that somewhere out there, there are people who actually enjoy reading my books. Anyway, I would super appreciate it, thanks.

If you see new books from me in the future, you will know that I wrote them because of your support. Thank you for supporting my work.

Special thanks again to previous readers and reviewers. Thank you for encouraging me to keep writing. I'll do my best to provide high quality books for you all.

My Other Books

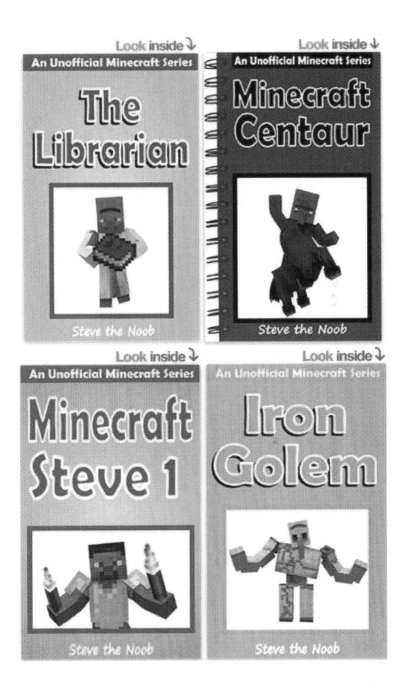

More Books

My Awesome List of Favorite Readers and Reviewers

W. shi "Jenn"

K.K "mysweetdees"

Mikail

WarCenturion

Stephanie Linn

Thank you so much for your support. You guys and girls rock!!

Jewel Shine

Minoscreeperslayer

RainbowCreeper

Sang Chul Choi

Misahti

Panisara W.

Astro Cat

AthanEnder

betsy

akaherobrine

James

Xaxier Edwards

leann xiao

Awesomeguy27

IsaBear556

Emma Hogan

Brandon Kim

Venu Gopal

Kathy

Yuan Cui

Sreekant Gottimukkala

Emma

Kayla Dingo

ZombieCupcake

Ding Zhou

Alex

spark527

Gator

Nick

devlin

Grant

MeowLord

Ducky MooMoo

Minecarft Book Girl

Jax/Blaze7381

Steve

Toni

Jane

Jacob

Dante

Skyler

Kayla Ding

nicole

shard

Cole

TheGolem64

JoshieWoshie12

Rosi

jhkim

Catboy327

Flamenarrow

MinerAwesomeGuy

Tommy

Teslageek

Calvin

Sid

J. Lada

Jason Hollister

TruReader

NinjaBoy899

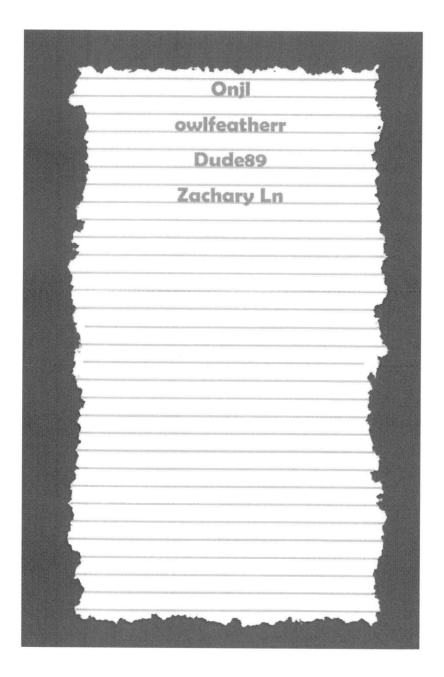

Onjl

owlfeatherr

Dude89

Zachary Ln

Made in the USA
Columbia, SC
14 September 2017